Charles R. Conybeare

Church Reform Movement at Rome

the Italian Catholic Church, Conte Enrico di Campello and Monsignore

Giambattista Savarese

Charles R. Conybeare

Church Reform Movement at Rome
the Italian Catholic Church, Conte Enrico di Campello and Monsignore Giambattista Savarese

ISBN/EAN: 9783337381486

Printed in Europe, USA, Canada, Australia, Japan

Cover: Foto ©Andreas Hilbeck / pixelio.de

More available books at **www.hansebooks.com**

CHURCH REFORM MOVEMENT AT ROME.

THE ITALIAN CATHOLIC CHURCH.

CONTE ENRICO DI CAMPELLO

AND

MONSIGNORE GIAMBATTISTA SAVARESE.

SECOND EDITION, with latest Information.

WINCHESTER :

PRINTED BY JACOB AND JOHNSON, HANTS CHRONICLE OFFICE.

PREFACE TO THE FIRST EDITION, 1883.

I would preface the following paper by saying that Count Enrico di Campello had been expected to attend the meeting* held at the house of Mr. E. Thornton, c.b., on the 11th of June last, but the services just commencing in the newly fitted Chapel of San Paolo detained him at Rome.

On the 6th of July Campello reached London at the invitation of Canon Meyrick, the honoured and indefatigable Secretary of the Anglo-Continental Society, and by him he was, on the Archbishop's invitation, taken to Lambeth, and was also introduced to many other dignitaries of our Church.

The paper which follows was read by me at a meeting on behalf of the Church reform movement at Rome, held in the house of Bishop McDougall, at Winchester, over which the Lord Bishop of that Diocese presided.

It was again read in Dean Plumptre's hall at Wells, to a meeting over which presided the Bishop, Lord A. Hervey.

The Count was present at both meetings, and spoke shortly in Italian. He said :—"As at the end of the sixth century Gregory the Great sent Augustine in the holy name of brotherhood to England as Missionary, so now he, a son of Rome, came in the 19th century to ask the same brotherhood from us. The national resurrection, and the recovery of civil rights at Rome, inspired the hope that her Church might also recover what she had lost of freedom and of the purity of her ancient faith. That loss had begun with her pretension to an universal episcopate, a claim rejected and anathematised by Gregory the Great, but now pushed to the insane demand for infallibility recently decreed as inherent in the Pope. Campello trusted that the Church of England would give a brother's helping hand to the Church of Italy, now awakening from her long lethargy, and aiming at a reformation, in many respects like that which had been brought about in England—a work

---

* See in the Appendix a notice of this Meeting from the *Guardian*.

not of innovation or destruction, but of restoration and conservation. He quoted the words of Bishop Wordsworth, spoken in favour of Italy at a meeting in London of the Anglo-Continental Society, when Bishop Wordsworth said :— 'I am perfectly certain that there are hundreds and thousands of men remarkable for piety and intelligence in Italy, who will soon take part in the movement of reform, and may God grant that they may succeed.' "

The Count's complete ignorance of English allowed me to speak freely—though in his presence—of the man himself, as well as of the work.

C. R. CONYBEARE.

Itchen Stoke Rectory, July 26th, 1883.

PREFACE TO SECOND EDITION.

My first edition of 500 copies has been widely distributed in England and America, and, at the request of many friends of the movement, I print now a second edition of 600 copies, adding the later history of the Italian Catholic Church at Rome.

I may say that I have this year spoken to the same effect at a meeting in Bournemouth in February under the presidency of the Bishop of Meath, Lord Plunket; and also in April at St. Leonard's, where the Bishop of Chichester presided.

C. R. CONYBEARE.

Itchen Stoke, Nov. 1, 1884.

CHURCH REFORM MOVEMENT AT ROME.

THE history of the Church reform movement at Rome, and of the Italian Catholic Church now in active life there, must begin with some account of him who, as its ordained priest, first ministered to the Congregation there.

Count Enrico di Campello,*whose family has been settled at Spoleto since the 8th century, is the second son of Count Solon, an intimate friend of Mastai Feretti, the then very liberal Archbishop of Spoleto. Under the Roman Republic Count Solon took office. On the return from Gaeta of his old friend—now Pope Pius IX., but no longer a Liberal—he fell into disgrace, whereby the ruin of the family fortunes was completed.

A reconciliation with the Pope was subsequently brought about on the condition that Count Solon should give up his son Enrico, then in his 22nd year, to the service of the Church ; and he, after studying theology and law, was, in 1855, ordained priest,

* Readers are referred for a fuller account of these matters to a very able article of Dr. Nevin, Rector of the American Church at Rome, entitled "A Notable Secession from the Vatican."—*Nineteenth Centn~y*, April, 1882.

together with the now Cardinals La Valetta, Oreglia, and Howard. Though made a priest more through the strong pressure of others than through his own desire, Count Enrico held high ideas of a priest's duty, and he gave himself at once to the work, taking charge of a mission to the sailors on the Ripa Grande, and of the work at the Oratory of the Ignorantelli.

After six years of this work the Pope made him Canon of the patriarchal Basilica of S. Maria Maggiore, and as such he continued in charge of the mission until his brother Canons—jealous of his youth and of his doing work outside the Basilica—virtually compelled him to give it up.

He then took the direction of a night school for workmen, and many of those who were then his pupils now tell how there was no school like it, no director so much loved as Campello. In confirmation of this I may mention that, shortly after the committee had hired the rooms now used as the Chapel of S. Paolo, Campello came to see about the needful alterations. Directly the lessor saw him he said, " Is the place for your use, Count Campello ? for if it be, I will only be paid for the materials used in the alterations, and not for the work, because I owe to your night school and to your teaching my present position and success in life."

This work at the night school, too, after nine years, had to be unwillingly surrendered to vexatious opposition; from which, however, the Pope rescued Campello by removing him to the Vatican as Canon of S. Peter's Basilica. Nor did he as such give up the real work he loved. He restored the small Church of S. Maria, near the Tarpeian rock, held services there every evening, and preached three times a week.

Nobly born, well taught, of much ability, of high character, and of winning manners, the young Canon had well within his reach every ecclesiastical honour, but his thoughts were busy about other things. I will say nothing of the years of disappointment that followed, in which he learned how hopeless was that reform within the Roman Church, upon which he had more and more set his heart.

At length, " after long strugglings," he was, as he says, " constrained by the grace of God to leave the ranks of the Roman clergy, that he might fight thenceforth in those of the pure Gospel of Christ, and be able to profess himself a Christian without hypocrisy, and an Italian citizen without the mask of a traitor to his country."

While in the Romish Church Campello's life gave proof of zeal for Christ's work ; and the sacrifice which he made for Christ's truth in leaving that Church must command the admiration of every generous nature. For, with a sister and a nephew dependent upon him, he gave up his canonry (then £500 and soon to be £600 a year), which was literally *all* his living ; he exchanged a most honoured position for contempt and hatred ; the most brilliant prospects, for a future uncertain even of food and clothing ; and he sacrificed almost all his old friendships—a sacrifice which to a celibate ecclesiastic of his affectionate nature means more than it could mean to us. Truly did he write under the photograph which he gave to me, " Straniero tra i miei," a stranger amongst mine own people.

The bitterness caused by Campello's renunciation of Rome was at once shown by the false accusations invented, not by his fellow Canons, but by the lower creatures of the Vatican ; and still colported by those

perverts from our own Church who congregate at
Rome, and repeated by many whose ignoble nature
likes better to accuse falsely, than freely to admire an
excellence that could never be their own. I have examined, but found no truth in any of these stories. Dr.
Nevin's fuller knowledge holds them false through-
out.* Monsignor Savarese, when Campello left the Vatican, while reprobating that move, wrote of him as
"a nobleman not wanting in learning, and of
unspotted life and reputation;" adding "I speak
from personal knowledge of Count Campello, and
in accordance with the reputation which he enjoyed
at Rome up to the time of his deplorable step;" and
that Cardinal whom Englishmen will most trust, told
a friend of mine that nothing of such kind could
be truly said against Campello. I have known him
intimately for six months at Rome, and I declare that
there could not be a more thorough gentleman, that
he is pure and high-minded, of simple, affectionate,
and winning nature, devout and zealous for Christ's
work.

On leaving the Vatican, Count Campello,
misled by the title " Episcopali," read the letter of
renunciation, which he had written to the Archpriest
of St. Peter's, in the Chapel of the "Metodistici
Episcopali"† at Rome, under the guidance of its very

---

* Dr. Nevin's most interesting article in the *Nineteenth
Century* of April, 1882, goes fully into these false charges. My
own examination of them was made during my last stay in Rome,
where I spent the two last months of 1882 and the four first
months of 1883. The utter want of scruple in Jesuit hostility is
sure to renew covertly these attacks, but, as the movement is now
more led by Monsignore Savarese than by Conte Enrico, their
slanders (though equally false) will now have less influence on any.

† In 1784, shortly after the peace, Wesley consecrated
Thomas Coke, D.C.L., a presbyter of the Church of England, to be
Bishop in the Southern Provinces of North America, whence

able and most excellent pastor, the Rev. Dr. Vernon, from whom he accepted for a while paid missionary work. But, on finding that the body was not truly episcopal, he separated from them, repaying that which he had received to Dr. Vernon, who still continues Campello's friend.

Dr. Nevin (colonel in the anti-slavery war, and for some ten years past Rector of St. Paul's, the noble American Church at Rome) now returned ; and from thenceforth Campello has acted with the advice of his old friend. Dr. Nevin is the ablest representative of our Anglo-American Church at Rome, and he knows, from intimacy with all sorts and conditions of Italians, more about their religious needs and feelings than does any other man. Application was now made by Campello himself to the Archbishop of Canterbury, between whom and Dr. Nevin there followed some correspondence, and it was finally decided, as Count Campello was a weekly communicant at the American Church, that for this and other reasons he had better be placed under an American Bishop. The Archbishop, then, as Chairman of the Pan-Anglican Committee, requested the Chairman of the Sub-committee of American Bishops to undertake the matter, and to supply by their Bishop of Foreign Affairs episcopal sanction, direction, and control to these formerly Romish priests, until such time as they might have a Bishop of their own. The Bishop of Long Island,

---

arose the Episcopal Methodists there. When Campello found, on inquiry, that this was the origin of their episcopate, he objected that Wesley, while a man of great holiness and of genius, was himself no Bishop; and that a true Bishop could only be made through men who were themselves Bishops. Then they alleged S. Paul; to which Campello replied, "Truly he was a Bishop made through no man, but, as the other Apostles, by Christ himself."

to whom the supervision of Campello's work was thus
delegated, has issued his official licence to Count
Campello, authorising him to exercise his office as a
dispenser of the Word of God and of His holy
Sacraments.*

So much as to the workman. Let me now speak of
the work, which is being carried out on thoroughly
Church lines. On the 8th of December, 1882, I was
present in Dr. Nevin's rooms at a meeting of Italians.
Count Campello (who read a paper), some half-dozen
other excommunicated † priests, some professors, and
some laymen of position, discussed the bases of a
reformed Church in Italy. They agreed that the
teaching and worship of the Wesleyans, Baptists,

---

* See in the Appendix the letter of Dr. Nevin on Campello's
ecclesiastical status written to the *Guardian*. See also the account
from that paper of a meeting held at the house of Mr. E. Thornton,
in Warwick Sqare, on the 11th of June last.

† One of the priests told me his story. Very many years
ago he was impressed by the discrepancy of much at Rome with
Christ's teaching as he read it in the Gospels; and he thought—
good simple man—that all would be corrected if he called attention to it. So he wrote a book and sent it to the Pope, to the
head of the Inquisition, and to Napoleon III., then, as he imagined,
all-powerful at Rome. Of course he was at once brought before
the Inquisition, and, vainly appealing to the Crucified One, who
was painted on the wall near the seat of his judges, was
condemned and led down to the dungeons of the Vatican. Taken
thence after a few years he was consigned to the gentler
custody of an Abbot, who, attracted by the old man's
goodness, allowed him to walk in the garden of the
Abbey. And now the Italian Government seemed likely to
be ere long in Rome, and very stringent measures were decided
upon at the Vatican against all recalcitrants. Of this the
friendly Abbot warned his prisoner, and advised a hasty escape
from his garden. The poor man escaped to Milan, and when
the Italians entered Rome returned an excommunicated priest,
to work partly as shopman, partly as porter, in a hardware store
at Rome.

Episcopal Methodists, and Waldensians, each and all failed to satisfy Italian needs, which craved, they said, a CHURCH, one historically with the Apostolic Church of Italy in doctrine, practice, and liturgy, purged only from modern errors, and restored to that which it was in the time of S. Ambrose—a Church, with the two Sacraments, the three orders, and with bishops of true Apostolical succession, having the Bible and liturgy in the vulgar tongue, with the cup restored to the laity, with confession, and also celibacy of the clergy, only voluntary, ready to acknowledge the Bishop of Rome as Bishop, but not as Pope. This meeting was not directly connected with that which followed, but I mention it to show the Church spirit which prevailed. I may note that a similar spirit seems to be widely at work in the Old Catholic movement of Germany and of France, in that of Switzerland under Bishop Herzog, and partly also in Spain, Portugal, and Mexico.

Active work at Rome in this matter originated with a large meeting held in Miss Mayor's house— a lady to whose generous and vigorous help the cause is largely indebted. At this meeting America, England, and, to some extent, Italy were represented. Count Campello read a paper on the nature of the Church work which he wished to do, and some there present were asked by the meeting to act as a committee for the organization of the work.

Rooms, far too small for the purpose, were taken in an out-of-the-way street near Santa Maria Maggiore, and these were fitted up, one as a night school, and the other for services and religious conferences, and so the S. Paul's Mission was started. Count Campello, assisted by another priest, began both night school and services, in which an Italian translation

8

from the Anglican Prayer Book was provisionally*
used, with the lessons read and sermons preached in
Italian. Accompanied by the harmonium, the canticles
were chanted and hymns sung, especially those
which have been translated by the late venerated
Count Tasca, whose work in North Italy is so well
known. There was, however, no celebration of
the Holy Communion, because Campello felt that this
should not be till he held episcopal licence. Congregations of from 25 to 35 gathered, and about half
that number were regular attendants, amongst whom
were several educated Italians.

Campello had had practice in preaching, and
proved an acceptable and effective preacher, but in
all his sermons there was not ever heard an attack
on Romish doctrine, except so far as clear statements
of a truth may be called an attack on its opposite
error.

Canon Thornton, after attending these services,
wrote, "no one who has heard Campello's graphic
and earnest sermons can doubt that he may be of the
greatest use; and no one who has seen the eager faces
of the men listening to the story of our Lord, read for
the first time before them in their own language, can
doubt the value of such services, if they can be
continued." Thus even in an unfitting home, the
Mission, considering all things, prospered fairly.

---

* I say provisionally, because the desire of Italians is not for
an Anglo-American, but for a native Italian Prayer Book, such
as would be formed by an expurgated translation and recension
from their own National Liturgies. I believe myself that we may
look forward to the help hereafter of one whose learning and
ability is competent to make such a recension and translation.
There exists already a beautiful translation of the Psalms—
accurate, rythmical, and in poetical language—by the Venerable
Padre Curci, which might, I believe, be (with his tacit consent)
cheaply reprinted in England for Italian use.

Campello gained valuable training for the work, and many who had hopelessly broken with Rome gained hope of the Church communion for which they longed.

After five months of patient work, in rooms too small, too unseemly, and too remote in situation to gather any but very small congregations, more spacious and seemly quarters have been found leading out of the central Via Nazionale. There a long room has been very decorously fitted up as S. Paul's Chapel, and now looks very churchlike. Close by, is a large room for the night school, and a small one for the custode priest. An organist has in training an efficient choir, drawn from the night school of forty lads, who are taught by Campello, and the Priest Loffredo, an ex-Franciscan, a good teacher of drawing and painting, and an able man. Another ex-frate in priest's orders, Signor Panzani, completes the staff, aiding Campello in preaching, and of Panzani's sermons I have heard recently from educated Italians high praise.

I may as well here answer some questions which have been asked concerning the movement for Church Reform in Rome. On one side it has been said to me—"I hope Campello's faith is more than negative, that it does not consist chiefly in repudiation of Romish error." To this I can reply of my own knowledge, gained from the hearing, and from the reports of his sermons, and from long talks with himself, that Campello's faith is very positive indeed; identical, I should say, with that of our most respected High Churchmen, and with that taught of old by our Anglo-Catholic divines; and that the movement is in respect to doctrine almost identical with that of the "Old Catholics."

On the other hand I have been asked—"Does Campello teach transubstantiation, Mariolatry, and prayers to the Saints?" Here again, of my own knowledge, similarly gained, I can reply that Campello does not teach or hold any of these doctrines.

He no way believes in the miracle of Bolsena, or in the material presence implied by transubstantiation, but in a very real presence of a spiritual nature.

With regard to the worship of the Blessed Virgin, I should like to say that those who have been born and bred in the Romish Church should meet with very tender treatment. The true Christ has—as Curci has said—been very little made known to them, and they have been taught, by the oral teaching now current, to look to His mother as the one source of all sympathy to man; and it must be painful to tear up by the roots the clinging worship so implanted. This worship of the Virgin has never been carried so far as in the latter days of Pius IX.; but not without sometimes rousing remonstrant feeling. A learned Monsignore, speaking of addresses to his clergy made by the present Pope while Archbishop and as yet free from domination of the Jesuits, said "these addresses are very good, the pet Madonna of Pius IX. (la Madonella di Pio Nono) is not to be seen, hidden by the majestic figure of Christ which fills all." And so it must be; the teaching of the true Christ must obliterate the false teaching of the Madonna; and Campello has himself learned, and teaches others, to know Christ as giving fullest sympathy to His brethren, as giving freest access to the Father for all His children, so that there is no possible room left for either worship of the Virgin, or prayers to the Saints.

Another question has been asked. "Is not Campello's Church Reform movement at Rome schismatical?" I ask, in reply, are we schismatical because we, for reasons less cogent—the Vatican decrees not then existing—separated from Rome?

On whom does the guilt of schism rest; on those who by enforcing scandalously false doctrine make separation inevitable, or on those who are thereby forced to separate, but who would gladly remain in their Church if not forced to accept, as the condition of communion, palpably false doctrines, and who are *ipso facto* excommunicated because they have done their duty as Italian citizens?

Whose are the preposterous claims that have caused all schisms, that between East and West, between Papistical and Reformation Churches, between Infallibists and Old Catholics? "No man," said a devout Monsignore, "can now hold office in our communion but by acknowledging the Pope as God?"*

Many thousands in Rome are refused communion because they have been loyal to king and country : as many, because they will not profess to their confessors their own faith in an irrational Immaculate Conception, and in the monstrous dogma of Infallibility. Are these thousands to be left to drift into utter infidelity, and to be sacrificed to the punctilious observance of the Church law against schism, which then only can be binding when the Church is herself obeying the infinitely higher law of teaching God's truth? Surely He favourably

---

* That is the truth forcibly expressed by the "Pasquinade" placarded at the time of the Infallibility decree :—

"*Quando Eva morse, e morder fece il pomo,*
Per salvar l' uomo, DIO si fece uomo ;
Ma, il Vicario di Cristo il nono Pio,
Per far schiavo l' uomo, si fece Dio !"

"When Eve ate, and made Adam eat the apple,
To save man, GOD made himself man :
But the Vicar of Christ, Pius the Ninth,
To make man a slave, made himself God."

allows the charitable work of Campello, who is supplying under episcopal guidance Church communion to those who, through no fault of their own, are excommunicated, and who have *already hopelessly broken* with the corrupt Papal Church.

This movement is, as I have said, not aggressive. It is no *direct** attack on Rome, nor does it seek to injure the Romish Church. In such aim *I* could not join ; for the Romish Church, with all its errors, must be for long the main barrier which protects the uneducated masses in Italy from materialism.

But as education spreads, and as men think more, the number is ever growing of those who—unable to accept the enforced teaching of the Vatican—crave a place in such a Church movement as this is. Nor will this movement be, in the end, without an influence from outside, upon that movement from inside the Roman Church, which has shown itself of late in the noble work of Padre Curci and others.

The movement does not aim at making proselytes, but only seeks to provide a Church as a city of refuge for those "who"—as our late Bishop Wilberforce writes—"have been led to break the enforced Roman obedience, and who wish to resume, as a branch of the Church Catholic, the primitive faith and practice."

And there are very many such amongst educated Italians, especially amongst those many officials who have lately come from the northern provinces to settle in Rome. Of these there is a large and

---

* This feeling is expressed in their subsequent answer to the Papal excommunicatory attack, where they say, "we are not trying to raise doubts in the mind of those who are not troubled with any contradiction between their religious and political faith (*i.e.* between religion and loyalty to their country). Our work of vital import is to gather and care for the faithful who cannot stand this contradiction."

increasing number who have been compelled by the anti-patriotic attitude of the Roman Curia to consider their position with regard to the Papal Church, and who have found it impossible to accept the recent decrees of the Vatican, and also in many cases some of the older decrees of Trent.

These men, virtually excommunicated by the Pope, are churchless. They have tried, as one of them (if I rightly remember, an ex-minister of State) said, to live a Christian life without a Church, but, having found that all but impossible, now crave a place in a branch of the Church Catholic which maintains the primitive faith and practice.

Some Romans I myself know, and I have heard of many more, who are in this condition. Some few have already found what they seek in the Church of which Campello is minister. More are coming in, and still larger numbers are waiting, with the exceeding caution of Italian nature, till they can see a large and stable body which they may join. Such a body would, I feel convinced, be at once seen, if only one-tenth part of those so waiting had the courage of their opinions. It is because this movement supplies a city of refuge from Nothingarianism and Materialism to educated Italians who have already hopelessly broken with Rome, that I have done all the little I could do to help it.

The condition of such men is dangerous and pitiable, and is not of their own seeking, but forced upon them by the cruel tryanny of Rome. Are not we, of a pure Apostolic Church, bound to help these, our shipwrecked brethren in Italy? Shall we stand on our own safe shore, and carelessly watch their struggle? Surely we ought, even at some loss to our-selves, to do what we can to help. And help is sorely needed now from our Church in England and America.

The priests in charge must be paid, because they have all, like Campello, in leaving Rome, stripped themselves of *everything*. Nor can the educated Italians, who have as yet joined and are joining, do much to help. They belong mostly to the middle class, whose income is in general no larger than that of our own bettermost artizans. An upper Government clerk, whose salary with us would be four or five hundred a year, receives in Italy but ninety pounds yearly. In five or six years the movement will, I hope, become self-supporting, but for the next five years large help must come from England and America. Without such help the successful and promising beginning of which I have tried to tell will be doomed by our want of love to ruinous collapse.

POSTSCRIPT.

On Saturday, December 8, 1883, Mgr. Savarese (created Prelato Domestico by Pius IX., and for 26 years a member of the Segnatura di Giustizia) sent in his resignation to the Cardinal Secretary of State. After abjuring the additions to the Creed made by the Council of Trent, together with the dogmas of the Immaculate Conception and Papal Infallibility, he was next day received at the Holy Communion by Dr. Nevin in St. Paul's Church, Rome.

In his letter of resignation Savarese says :—" No rancour or personal disappointment has caused my determination. A profound conviction, long combated, but never vanquished, compels me to take this step, necessary to the spirit, but grievous to the flesh, fearing, as I do, that I shall lose the friendship of excellent companions whose old prejudices may prevent them ever again shaking hands with me."

He wishes, he says, to devote his remaining strength to the service of religion and his country. He feels that the Curia cannot be brought back to the mark ; while pressing social, moral, political, and economical necessities require the religion of Christ to be restored to its original principles, that by such renovation it may regain its former repute, and power of growth.

Savarese's application for Episcopal guidance was made, Dr. Nevin says,* to the Archbishop of Canter-

---

* See Dr. Nevin's letter to the *Guardian* on Savarese's step— Appendix C.

bury as head of the Commission appointed by the Lambeth Conference in 1878, to deal with such cases. His Grace, for reasons of convenience, referred it to the Bishop in charge of the American chapels on the continent of Europe, in like manner as the application of the Count di Campello had been referred to the same Bishop by our late Archbishop Tait. Thus Mgr. Savarese will work for the restoration of the primitive faith and Catholic order in the Church of Italy, under due Episcopal guidance and protection.

The following words were written in a letter then sent by me to the *Guardian* newspaper :—

"By the secession from the Vatican of Mgr. Savarese a most notable addition has been made to the number of those who—as the late Bishop Wilberforce wrote—have been led to 'break the enforced Roman obedience, and are seeking to resume, as a branch of the Church Catholic, the primitive faith and practice.'

"Such an ally and leader for the Church Reform movement at Rome is, I know, the fulfilment of Count Campello's dearest wish ; and I believe that the power, learning, ability, and judgment of Savarese, joined to the energy, single-hearted love, and eloquence of Campello, will give to that movement a leading and management of the most perfect.

"To follow Christ, Savarese, like Campello, has given up all, and passes from wealth to absolute poverty. Surely those who can will aid the funds of this movement, so that a brother who has ventured all for Christ, and who is still working for Him, may be kept above actual want."

Mgr. Savarese, his father's eldest son, was born December, 1829, on a small estate at Vico-Aquense, in the Sorrentine Peninsula. His early teacher was a relative, Rector of the Seminary there, Donato Savarese, a good Latinist and Theologian. When sixteen Savarese was placed under the best teachers at Naples, and he was ordained Priest just before his twenty-third year, devoting himself to work in barracks, military hospitals, and prisons, and doing much for the young students of the Belle Arti.

He was also a most diligent student and German scholar, and wrote many notable reviews and some books. In 1859 he published *L' Introduzione alla Storia Critica della Filosofia dei SS. Padri*, the broader views of which alienated his friend, Sanseverino, and won the ill-will of the Jesuits.

Soon after this his health failed, and he went to Rome. There he was, before long, nominated Prelato Domestico of Pius IX., and became ·Doctor of Canon and Civil Law in the Roman University. He then took the oath as Referendario of the Supreme Tribunal at Rome, and was much occupied in the more important causes of that Court.

He was an intimate friend and fellow-workman of the most illustrious Clerics of the Vatican; and Pius IX. held him in the highest esteem, and employed him largely on various important matters, appointing him one of the committee of sixteen for preparation of the Syllabus, and there in his case, as in that of three others, the studies for that subject led the way ultimately to severance from the Vatican.

Savarese was a close friend and defender of Curci, and in answer to the Jesuits' reply to Curci's "*La Nuova Italia ed i vecchi Zelanti*," wrote his "*Moderna Civiltà difesa*." Many other books he wrote, showing much learning and great literary power; and three months after he left the Vatican he delivered in the Sala Dante at Rome, to a very numerous and most interested audience, three most able lectures on "I beni Ecclesiastici."

Savarese is everywhere most highly respected, and his name carries with all Italians great weight, so that his joining Campello as chief leader of the Chiesa Cattolica Italiana, has given lifeful strength and firm solidity to that Church.

I said in the earlier* part of this paper that the Italians desired a native Italian Prayer Book, formed by an expurgated translation and recension of their own National Liturgy; and that I then believed we might look forward to the help of one whose learning and ability was competent to make both a recension and translation. Savarese's coming has fulfilled this hope. He at once prepared such a recension of the Sunday Service, and has now just brought out in Italian the full Liturgy of the Italian Catholic Church, an expurgated translation of the Missal, in nearly 200 large octavo pages of close printing.

Thus the Italian Catholic Church at Rome had all that it needed for life and growth. A complete Italian Liturgy, a seemly Church in the Chapel of S. Paolo, a learned and able Rector† and Vicar in Savarese and Campello, and two excellent Curates in Fr. Andrea and Cicchitti.

The last named, Cicchitti, is a young man of considerable ability, who was under instruction for the priesthood by the Jesuit College at Rome, and had in 1881 been ordained sub-deacon. Having later in that year read Curci's *La Nuova Italia ed i Vecchi Zelanti*, and the Jesuits' reply, and having studied also the answer to that reply in Savarese's *Civiltà Moderna Difesa*, Cicchitti became convinced of the errors taught by the Jesuits in his College, and gave his adhesion to the reform movement under Savarese and Campello, and was received as a member of the Catholic Italian Church.

---

* Note to Page 8.

† They do not bear these English titles, which I only use to make the matter clear to the English reader.

Shortly after he was sent to the Old Catholic College at Berne, and, having been subsequently ordained full deacon and priest by Bishop Herzog, he returned to work in the Chapel of S. Paolo at Rome. There the services went on, and the steady congregation was slowly increasing, when, by the Pope's order, the Cardinal Vicar, on the 29th of September, 1884, published, and ordered to be read, and explained, in all parishes, on some festival, his notification that the greater excommunication rested upon all who had anything whatsoever to do with the Chapel of S. Paolo, whose practices and doctrines he violently attacked.

"Its leaders arrogate," he said,* "the title of Catholic Italian Church, being neither Catholic nor Italian; they parody every Sunday the Divine mysteries, destroying discipline by their unauthorised alterations. They do away with the special language of the Church, of the Fathers (!) and of the Councils, (!) replacing it with a jargon which no true Italian could recognize. These improvised apostles presume to speak in God's name without being sent; whereas the Priest rightfully is dependent on the Bishop, who glories in his own subjection to the Pope, to whom alone Christ committed the flock entirely, without limit or reserve. They abandon St. Peter's Chair, on which the Church is founded, and so cannot pretend to belong to the Church. They are heretics in holding communion with the old Catholics, and rejecting the jurisdiction and infallibility of the Pope. They adjudge the schismatical Eastern and Anglican Churches to be parts of the true Church. They attack the †priests' power to remit and retain sin, and teach a spiritual and not the true material, real presence in the Eucharist."

---

* This short abstract of the Vicar General's accusation is more forcible, I think, than the somewhat wordy and wandering original, the language of which is contemptuous and insulting. It calls, for instance, Savarese's Italian "*gergo non riconoscibile dal Cavalca* (I suppose the Cardinal meant Cavalcanti) *nè dall' Alighieri*," and calls the S. Paolo flock, not "*congregazione*," but "*congrega*," which means a meeting of men for evil purposes, &c.

† The Cardinal quotes here from the Italian translation of our Anglican absolution, which translation of our service was only provisionally in use at S. Paolo's Chapel, while their Liturgia was being translated.

The Vicar-General also specifically attacked their Liturgy, which, as it had not then been published, he could never have seen.

This attack ended with the declaration that all adherents, attendants, and visitors, and all who in any way whatever assisted S. Paolo's services, incurred the major excommunication, from which they could only be absolved by the Pope himself.

An immediate reply was at once given to the Cardinal Vicar's attack, and published in the *Labaro*, Campello's fortnightly journal——"The organ of Catholic reform in Italy"——as the answer* of the Italian Catholic "Congregation at Rome" addressed

TO THE ITALIANS.

All men know the declaration of most severe ecclesiastical censure, which has been furiously hurled by the orders of the Holy Father against our Catholic Church of the Via Genova, under the pretext and imputation of schism, breach of discipline, and heresy.

For its most bitter style, hateful, outrageous, and over-bearing words, we do not care at all, because we can pardon fanatic zeal for the offence done to us ; but we cannot keep silence as to the errors, which are hurtful to all.

---

*I print here my full translation of the reply as more true than the necessarily altered order of an abstract would be. To our northern mind the reply may seem to want something of condensation, and force ; but it will be very telling with Italians, and, after the close attention required in translating it, I like it much better than I did when I first read it. Savarese's answer to the Cardinal Vicar of Rome, " the excommunication of an idea," is now printed, and is a very learned and vigorous work of 97 pages, very well worth reading. It is a thorough answer to the Cardinal Vicar, and a crushing exposition of the false claims of the Papacy. They have forced most of the booksellers at Rome to remove this book of Savarese's from their shop windows.

It is not our cause which is in question, it is not our good name which is hurt; a speculative truth is not debated, nor a practice of private or public life. The salvation of souls—the religion of the people, which Peter and Paul first taught to the Romans, and a thousand Martyrs sealed with their blood is, indeed, at stake.

If Vatican superstition must weigh eternally on Italian necks, if—as the Curia affirms—there cannot be an escape from absolute obedience to the Curia, save in rushing to the lowest depths of impiety, Italy must, by the inexorable laws of logic, abjure science, say good-bye to liberty, deny the rights of reason, renounce the peaceable evolution of public life, resign itself to the condition of a degraded and outworn civilization, as true civilization is cursed by infallible Popes and condemned by the Syllabus. Liberty of the press and of conscience, the people's vote, the representative form of government, and even the unity of our country, are looked upon as errors and most pestilent heresies, which the Pope cannot possibly absolve, because he is obliged to avoid contradicting the dogma of Vatican infallibility. No link of the chain riveted on our neck by the Curia—which is enslaved to the blackest sect—can possibly be unfastened or broken; and he who does not lie to God, to himself, and to his confessor, by pretending to believe the absurd dogma of a Divine prerogative bestowed on the chosen of the Cardinals, must for all his days live deprived of the Sacraments, and be robbed even in death of the last comforts of religion.

And just as much as agreement between civilization and the Papacy seems to us impossible (now that the Papacy has made itself one with the fatal

Company), just so much does the harmony of science and liberty with the Universal Church seem to us possible and certain.

The Roman Church, according to Paul the Apostle,* is not the root (as it boasted to be from the beginning of its conversion), but is a branch, and that not a natural one, sustained by the only root, the Redeemer, who could as a punishment, when a branch became hurtful to the tree, cut it away. Now, if the root be holy, as St. Paul teaches, and the branches can be unholy through want of faith, we, even though excommunicated by the Curia, have the consciousness of being joined to the root and of participating—as St. Paul says—in the fatness of the olive. The Pope is not the Catholic Church, which existed even before the Gospel was preached at Rome.

The government of the Church is founded on the universal episcopate, to which, in the person of Peter, as St. Augustine teaches, Christ committed the feeding of His flock. And so long as we do not deny that the Bishops are true successors of the Apostles, we must reckon as sophisms the scholastic hard sayings by which Romanists maintain that all Bishops receive their mission from the Pope. Certainly to the Apostles and their successors the Saviour said, "As the Father hath sent me, so send I you." † The WE of the Pope is not of equal worth with the I of Incarnate Wisdom. According also to the teaching of Paul the Apostle to the Ephesians, it is Christ himself who, " having ascended into heaven, has provided Apostles for the Church, who were placed by the Holy Spirit as Bishops to rule the Church of God," ‡ and therefore St. Cyprian considered the episcopal office as ONE §

---

* Romans xxi., 18. † John xx., 28. ‡ Acts xx., 28.
§ De Unit. Eccl. c., v.

from which each Bishop holds his part of full episcopal right. The different episcopal seats, says St. Jerome, do not bring diversity of merit or of weight. The Bishop of Rome, or of Gubbio, of Constantinople, or of Reggio, have each the same priestly office, and are all of them successors of the Apostles. * This truth was too hot for the Legates at Trent, who imposed silence, and several Spanish Bishops and Doctors, more firm in upholding ancient discipline, were on their return proceeded against by the Holy Office. This, at least, touched the individuals ; the excommunication launched against us wounds, on the contrary, the Universal Church ; in schism from which the Curia declares itself to be by this ill-advised act.

Our mission, then, under present circumstances, comes to us from Bishops who have remained firm in the faith and in the discipline of the Catholic Church, as those of the venerable Eastern Churches (never subject to the Bishop of Rome), of the Anglican Churches, and of those in Holland, Germany, and Switzerland, who have had the courage to maintain the Catholic faith against papal usurpations.

This episcopate, certainly Catholic, reckoning us as Catholic priests, has given us the right of preaching the true Gospel, and of administering the sacraments to all who are firmly and faithfully attached to the pure faith of our fathers, and who, only because they refuse to go further and to believe the new dogmas, are deprived of the sacraments, and through them of the spiritual food of their souls.

Besides this Catholic Episcopate, learned and pious Bishops of Italy are feeling with us, whom the

---

* Ad. Evang. Ep., 148.

Jesuit spies and the explicit new dogmas' oath, are not sufficient to bind. All feel the most grave disturbance caused to the divine constitution of the Church by papal ambition ; by which from judges of the Faith, the Bishops have become, by the Pope's favour, advocates in the Papal Court : from equals, from brothers, each with his own full share of the one only episcopate—as St. Cyprian teaches—they have become inferiors, valets, and train-bearers of the Bishop of Rome, before whom they bend the knee, whose shoe they kiss, on the lowest step of whose throne they sit, and offer the service of acolytes : and a greater abasement—the Cardinals intruded into the Catholic hierarchy after a thousand years had passed, and set up in the saddest period of barbarism and of Ecclesiastical corruption, give, in their quality of Roman congregation prefects, masterful orders to the Bishops. Let us hasten by our prayers the moment, when our Bishops may be in a condition to show freely their own opinion in defence of the ancient discipline, chiefly in regard to Episcopal election, which our new times have made profitable and necessary. Towards this reformation most powerful aid will come to them from the people, having fullest faith in God, that Italy will not be wanting in her religious mission, and that the time will come— already prophesied by many—when each Church will shake off the Papal yoke, restoring the ancient discipline of election by the people. This, which was in vigour for twelve centuries, cannot fail to be renewed when the spirit reawakens in the multitude, and they acquire the consciousness of their rights in the Church—rights usurped, as Cardinal di Cusa teaches, but of which at any time they have the right to claim restoration.

Nor is the accusation of heresy worth more; from it we cleanse ourselves fully. Vincent of Lirins, a teacher not suspected by the Curia, warns that when a new error threatens the whole Church, it is needful to adhere to antiquity which is not subject to the frauds of innovators. And our judgment agrees with his, while we reason much as follows. In the Gospels, in which all is found that is necessary of belief for salvation, the Vatican additions do not exist. In the Nicene Council the jurisdiction of the Bishops of Rome is defined and limited to a district round the town measured by a hundred mile radius. The third general Council decreed the restoration of jurisdiction usurped over provinces not subject in ancient times. The Council of Chalcedon prescribed that the order of Ecclesiastical seats should accommodate itself to political changes. Finally the Council of Trent itself acknowledged and declared the Apostles' Creed to be in the Church the one foundation of faith universal. * We can therefore with the whole of antiquity remain Catholic, repudiating any extra belief in the new dogmas.

That alone is properly and fully Catholic according to Lirins, which in every place, by all men, and at all times has been held by the Church. † The personal infallibility of the Bishop of Rome is an addition made to the primitive faith as given by the General Council of Constance, and is contrary to the definition of the 2nd and 3rd of Constantinople, and of Basle confirmed by Eugenius IV.; and therefore, according to the 7th Canon of the Œcumenical Council of Ephesus, and to the decrees of the 4th General Council of Chalcedon, which forbid every addition, the Bishop of Rome has incurred the penalty of deposition.

---

* Concil Trident Sess, 3.   † Cont. Hæres, Cap. 3.

We then are not heretics because error contrary to
Catholic truth is absent; because there is absent any
intention of contradicting the certain definitions of
the Church, in which on the contrary we desire to
maintain pure the primitive belief.

The proofs, which the Cardinal Vicar falsely
brought forward in accusing our liturgy of heresy, fall
of themselves before the fact (almost incredible) that
this liturgy, which only came out to-day, could not
have been read by them; yet for all that, before it
was read it has been judged and condemned. It is a
manifest and open calumny to say that we deny to the
blessed Virgin Mary the august title of " Mother of
God," which is read in the very words of the Roman
Liturgy at our 5th page. It is a calumny to say that
we have withdrawn a single name of the Saints com-
memorated in the Canon. Yet we are generous and
do not ask them to make reparation for criminally discreditable charges made against us, not because im-
punity is granted for lying and calumny by Italian
law, but because we believers in Christ do not like to
contradict the Lord's prayer or His example.

Before those who are not troubled by the contradiction between their religious and * political faith we
put no scruples of any kind ; our work of most vital
import is only directed to welcome in the readiest and
widest way the faithful who cannot endure that contradiction. And to them we voluntarily administer
the sacrament, reassuring them that as we stand on
ancient ground, they can laugh at having the name of

---

* The meaning here is—we are not trying to raise doubts in the
minds of any who are not now troubled by the contradiction between their religion and their loyalty to their country. Our
vitally important work is to care for those faithful ones who find
themselves unable to stand that contradiction.

heretic pinned on to them, which better fits him who arrogates to himself, with sacrilegious blasphemy, the mission of Christ, who alone can say "I am the way. the truth, and the life." These have no fear of the stain of schism, because remaining in union with antiquity they cannot be separated from the Catholic Church. The appearance of rebellion against the Curia does not offend them, because there are circumstances which not only render it lawful (according to the Jesuit Bellarmine himself) but make it a duty, like the open opposition of Paul the Apostle to St. Peter ; and the opposition of St. Cyprian, of St. Augustine, of St. Ignatius, and of other Saints to the Bishops of Rome.

We understand that the Vatican policy would have pardoned us for some heresy, and would, perhaps, have further pardoned some little schism, if we had been washed clean of Italianity—a colour abhorred by the Pretender.

The public voice has pronounced what our true sin is in the eyes of the Curia, and the sour, stinging, scornful language in this part of the Notification gives evidence of a grave and sharp wound in their feelings. The prayer due for the king, the warm supplications for the independence, and for the greatness of our country, are sins that our "Congregazione" cannot pardon. But in us was no intention to affront any one ; there was not adhesion to any kind of political party. Our standard was to do honour to the august head of our nation, through religious duty, through citizens' duty ; above all, moreover, to love our country which, after God, comprehends all our loves, and in which by Divine Providence we were born men and citizens, before we became Sons of the Church. Oh! why in hatred of this our country, must that, which has been granted to others, be unlawful for us ? Pope John VIII. thought that the difference of language was fitted to give greater glory to the Divine Majesty, and one language alone was never the language of the Catholic Church, which, when gathered in its Councils, used Greek before it used Latin. Greek and Latin speech were introduced exactly at the time when they were the vulgar tongues, nor is there reason why our Italy should be robbed of that advantage which all other nations enjoy.

May God do away with the sad augury, that Italy, in deserting the old Curia, must rush to the lowest depths of impiety, just as it pleases the Cardinal Vicar to prophesy. The best answer to make him is, that all who feel an Italian soul within them, should know how to join in practice the feelings of free citizens with a sincere devotion to God, with attachment to the Catholic Church, with the incorrupted faith of our Fathers. Christ was the head of those excommunicated from the synagogue, and for that reason suffered outside the gate. With Paul the Apostle let us exhort the Italians to come out, to make themselves imitators of Christ without the gate :* there it will come to pass that we suffer insult ; but Christians know how to pardon in dying, and to fight so long as their life lasts for the truth and for the faith.

For the Italian Catholic Church.

MONSGR. GIAMBATTISTA SAVARESE.
CONTE ENRICO DI CAMPELLO.
FR. ANDREA D'ALTAGENE CAPNO.
SAC. FILIPPO CICCHITTI-SURIANI.

Rome, Oct. 17, 1884.

---

* Hebrews xiii., 13

The Cardinal Vicar's attack led very many more on the following Sunday to incur the major excommunication by crowding the chapel of S. Paolo. The second Sunday morning following a fair number were partakers of the Holy Communion, and at Vespers fifty—the seats being all filled—were standing.

"The formal excommunication launched by the Pope on the "29th of September against all the members of this Congrega- "tion has given them—writes* Dr. Nevin from Rome—a great "lift. It has not frightened away a single member of their "usual congregation; but it has drawn to their services many "new hearers. It has made their hopes and efforts known to "thousands all over Italy, who otherwise might never have "heard of them ; and it has generally awakened a kindly "disposition towards them. Many letters have come in from "Priests all over Italy, who, even if they are not so situated "as to be able to cast in their lot at once with this open move- "ment for reform, yet hearing these things, wish to say that "they thank God and take courage."

"The Press all over Italy has been led to take notice of the "stand now making for Catholic reform, and an opening has "thus come for a statement of its true principles and aims to "be brought before the Italian peoples."

The Vatican is angered and frightened, † and probably in the next encyclical the Pope will especially condemn the S. Paolo congregation and its priests : and perhaps there may follow an excommunication by name of the latter. The Jesuits, with their immense wealth, their widest influence, and their utter want of honest scruple, vigorous before in their

---

* See Dr. Nevin's letter to the *Guardian* in the Appendix D.

† I think the Vatican means vigorous action, for there has been of late hostility shown to the Alt Katholiks in Austria, and pressure against them in Germany. Doubtless the new elections will force Bismarck to seek the assistance of the Roman Catholic members, who will demand further concessions to the Vatican. The recent withdrawal by Curci of all words which have been condemned by the Index points I think to strong Vatican pressure upon him.

C

opposition, will now doubtless put forth all their strength to try and crush this hopeful movement for Church reform. Never has that been so hopeful as it now is; and never has it so much as now needed all the help that can be given to it by England and America.

It may certainly be said that the Italian Catholic Church at Rome has the sanction and approval of the English and of the American Church. Campello's application was kindly accepted by our late Archbishop Tait, who, as head of the Commission appointed by the Lambeth Conference, in 1878, to deal with such cases, advised that Campello should act under the supervision of the Bishop in charge of American Churches in Italy, and from that Bishop, Campello holds official licence. The present Archbishop followed the same plan with regard to Savarese, who is acting under like episcopal license. Our present Archbishop has shown much interest in the matter, and welcomed most kindly Campello when he was in England.

The Bishops of Winchester, of Chichester, of Bath and Wells, of Meath, and Bishop McDougall presided over meetings at which the cause was pleaded; and the Bishops of Lincoln, of Durham, and of Carlisle have, I know, shown sympathy, as have, I believe, many other Bishops.

The Anglo-Continental Society has taken up this cause, giving a large grant in aid of the printing of Savarese's Liturgia* ; and receiving, and placing to a special account at Messrs. Hoare's, subscriptions for the Italian Church Catholic, whence considerable sums have been sent to Rome.

There is very great need of larger help now.

---

* See Dr. Nevin's letter, Appendix E, on the Liturgia and the answer to the Cardinal Vicar's excommunication.

Savarese hopes that in one or two years aid may come largely from Italians; but at present foreign aid is needed not only to pay the stipends of those serving the Church at Rome, but almost certainly will soon be asked for Churches which the inhabitants in other Italian towns are wishing to set up.

Canon Meyrick, of Blickling Rectory, Aylsham, Secretary of the Anglo-Continental Society; Canon Thornton, Rector of Callington, Cornwall; and the Rev. C. R. Conybeare, of Itchen Stoke Rectory, Alresford, Hants, will do their best to answer any questions, and will forward to the Anglo-Continental Special Fund at Messrs. Hoare's any subscriptons that may be sent to them.

C. R. CONYBEARE.

I feel bound to add some reply to the discreditable accusation brought forward by *The Guardian* newspaper of October 29—against the founders of the Church Reform movement at Rome. I would refer the reader to page 4, where I mention the false accusations, made three years ago, against Count Campello on his leaving the Vatican, *not* by his fellow Canons, but by the lower creatures of the Vatican. I said that Dr. Nevin had carefully examined these accusations, and (as he told in his *Nineteenth Century* article, April, 1882,) had found them groundless; that I myself had examined them at Rome with the same result; that Monsignor Savarese, then a Prelate of the Vatican, wrote of Campello as one of " unspotted life and reputation;" that the Cardinal, most trusted by Englishmen, had said that nothing of the kind could be truly spoken against Campello.

I may now further add that in the Cardinal Vicar's late virulent attack, not the slightest hint of such an accusation was given. Most certainly no accusation has ever been breathed by any against Savarese.

The Paris correspondent of the *Guardian* had this information before him, and I think justice and truth should have made him pause before making himself the mouthpiece of his Ultramontane friends' libellous accusation.

He gives * an anonymous accusation, of unnamed crimes, against the ministers of St. Paolo's Chapel, and vouches for the honesty of the accusers.

Surely the editor should have at once cut out any mention of such an accusation, which he himself (see below) qualifies as libellous and condemns as anonymous.

See Dr. Nevin's answer Appendix F.

---

* "I think it right, says the *Guardian* Paris correspondent, in consequence of a letter from Rome (Dr. Nevin's Appendix D) which appears in your correspondence of last week, to send you a statement on the same subject, and from the same place, which, as you are aware, I received some time ago, but to which it did not then seem desirable or necessary to give publicity. But now, if adherence and co-operation with the movement in question is to be invited, it is certainly desirable that investigation into its origin and character should be invited also, and that members of our own Church at home should be enabled, as far as possible, *audire alteram partem*, before in any way committing themselves. It is with this view solely, and without the slightest intention of prejudging the matter in question one way or another—to do which I have neither sufficient means of information nor authority—that I transmit to you the following statement. I give it without vouching for anything further than that I believe it to be made with perfect good faith. But as it comes from a purely Roman source there can be no doubt that it is tinctured with Roman prejudices. [The letter that follows contains serious charges that ought not to be made anonymously. They are undoubtedly libellous, even if true.]"

APPENDIX A.

Notice from the GUARDIAN *of a Meeting, &c.*

On Monday, June 11, 1883, a meeting was held at the house of Mr. E. Thornton, in Warwick-square, for the purpose of giving information about the movement for religious reform in Italy, now being made by Count Enrico di Campello. Canon Thornton gave an account of Count di Campello's life and character. As a boy he had exposed the pretended miracle of the Winking Madonna. As a young man he had hesitated to be ordained, from the high standard he had set before himself, and his fear that he had not received the inward call of the Holy Spirit. When ordained he was wholly given to the work to which he had been called. His preaching attracted attention; his zeal in night schools and spiritual work amongst the young men of the working classes led to petty persecution from the other Canons of Sta. Maria Maggiore. What was thought of him was made clear by the early age at which he was moved to the dignified ease of a canonry of St. Peter's. Compelled by his high position to give up not only the night school work he loved, but even preaching, he only thought the more, and his chief friends were those in high places, who, like himself, longed for deliverance from the corruption and error in which they found themselves. For a considerable period he had hope of companions in the act of separating from the Papal Church; but at length he came out alone, sacrificing not only his large income and high position, but friends, family, and all means of living. At first he made two mistakes. He joined himself at first to the Methodists, believing them to be the Church in America; but he left them to put himself under Dr. Nevin, as soon as he found out his error. The other mistake was publishing his autobiography, and allowing it to be translated by an incapable hand. The playful and delicate irony with which an Italian attacks an evil became in a coarse translation the merest egotism, and it gave rise to a notion that it contained a confession that he had led an evil life; an impression for which the original afforded no foundation. Then he was persuaded, without sufficient capital or fit training, to publish a paper, with the natural consequence that he was left, not merely penniless, but burdened with a debt which would have been discharged by others, but that it seemed to him more personal than commercial. Then followed a time of positive want, with a sister and nephew wholly dependent upon him, from which he was not delivered till the return to Rome of English and American friends. Dr. Nevin, than whom there could not be a better witness, had with others investigated all the stories told against Count Campello, and had found that they had absolutely no foundation, while those of highest position in the Papal court, who were asked their opinion of him, declared that, except in his defection from them, there was not, and never had been, the slightest fault in his life or character. Dr. Nevin also testified to his life since he had been a communicant at the American Church, and no one who knew his simplicity, his pureness, his humility, his deep personal piety, could doubt that for long years he had been living in the Spirit of God. In the dark, out-of-the-way shop in which the services were first held, some souls were built up in their faith in Christ, and in the new chapel of St. Paolo there is a choir of more than five-and-twenty men and boys, and an increasing congregation. One of the ablest and most learned prelates of the Vatican, who had blamed Campello's action in leaving the Church of Rome, was now, under his influence, on the eve of following his example. But help was really needed. The little band of workers, two of whom had been in prison, one narrowly escaping death, for the sake of the truth, were wholly dependent upon the fund for which appeal was made; and at least £150 must be sent before the next season in Rome begins:

Mr. Theodore Bent then moved:—

"That this meeting is convinced that the movement for reform in the Church in Italy, begun by Count Enrico di Campello, has a claim upon the prayers and the help of other portions of the Church of Christ."

He (Mr. Bent) said he had been moved to take an interest in the work by what he had himself seen in Rome. He had attended some of the services, and been satisfied they were likely to supply the very want felt by educated Italians. The sermons were real and earnest, and the service neither cold and bare, nor crushed by an unintelligible ritual. He was anxious to do anything in his power to help a work so sure to meet successfully a great want. The Rev. C. R. Conybeare, in seconding this resolution, said he had known Count Campello intimately for the last six months, and could say from that personal knowledge that he was a pure, high-minded Christian gentleman, and one whose whole heart was in his work as a minister of Christ. He had taken pains to sift the stories told against him, and had found that they were wholly destitute of truth ; some, indeed, being so absurd as to carry with them their own refutation. He could speak, too, of his knowledge of the need of a reform on Church lines, and of the many Italians who were yearning for a purer faith and a less corrupt Church. He had gladly taken a part in this work, and was anxious to help it forward in any way in his power. The resolution was carried.

APPENDIX B.

Letter of Dr. Nevin on Count Enrico di Campello.
[FROM THE " GUARDIAN."]

SIR,—Many inquiries have been made to me this winter from England with regard to the Count di Campello, with the request that I should make public some authoritative statement of his present ecclesiastical *status* and work. Will you allow me to do so through your columns ?

First, as to Christian life and character. He has for the last year and a half attended faithfully the early celebration at St. Paul's Church, and received the Holy Communion with great regularity. During this time I have never seen in him, or heard in regard to his life, anything that was unbecoming a Christian profession. He has been thrown much during this time with several English clergymen who have passed the winter in Rome, all of whom will bear me out that, in a period of great hardness, trial, and disappointment, he has shown, if not great energy, yet certainly much patience, gentleness, and perseverance.

Secondly, as to his ecclesiastical *status*. He has consistently stood for Roman Catholic reform in the Church in Italy. When wrongfully cut off from the communion of the local Bishop, he turned in January, 1882, to the Catholic Episco-pate in communion with the see of Canterbury for Episcopal help and protection. The late Archbishop of Canterbury received his application most kindly, and, after giving the case his most earnest personal attention, finally advised that the Count di Campello should for the time being stand under the supervision of the Bishop in charge of the American Churches in Italy. The Bishop of Long Island, to whom the actual supervision of his work was thus delegated, has now issued to him an official licence in which he formally declares the excommunication of the priest, Enrico Count di Campello, by the Bishop of Rome, to be "utterly null and void," recognises him "as a priest in the Church of God," and authorises him—

"To execute his office as a ' dispenser of the Word of God, and of His Holy Sacraments,' working wherever there may be lawful opportunity for a reform of the Church in Italy, upon the model of the primitive Church,"

And in carrying out this work he is further authorised—

"Until such time as the service book of the Church in Italy can be duly revised, to make use provisionally of the forms of worship set forth by the Church in England and in America, or of so much of them as may be found needful, as well as of such part of the Latin uses as may be consistent with the faith and order of the truly Catholic and Apostolic Church."

This action of the Bishop of Long Island as a "Bishop in the Church of God" is explicitly founded upon the declaration on the subject of Catholic Reform set forth by "the hundred Catholic Bishops assembled at Lambeth, England, 1878," and the further affirmation of

"The Bishops of the Church in the United States of America assembled *in Council* as Bishops in the Church of God, New York, 1880. . . . . That the great primitive rule of the Catholic Church—*Episcopatus unus est, cujus a singulis in solidum pars tenetur*—imposes upon the Episcopates of all national Churches holding the primitive faith and order, and upon the several Bishops of the same, not the right only, but the duty also, of protecting in the holding of that faith and the recovering of that order those who have been deprived of both by the usurpations of the Bishop of Rome."

And, further, upon the facts that :—

"The Priest Enrico, Conte di Campello, has been cut off from his communion by the Bishop of Rome because he refuses to teach or to hold as of the Catholic faith the false dogmas which the Papacy has sought to impose upon the Catholic Church, by the decrees of the Councils of Trent and of the Vatican, and . . . has in this extremity appealed to the Catholic Episcopate in the Anglican Communion for ecclesiastical help and protection, in order that he may, with due authority, continue to labour for the preservation of the Catholic faith and the restoration of primitive order in the Church of Italy, and has given satisfactory evidence that he accepts, whole and entire, the Catholic faith as defined by the undivided Church."

And finally, that this application has been referred to the Bishop of Long Island " by the late Archbishop of Canterbury, Archibald Campbell Tait, D.D., D.C.L., acting as chairman of the commission appointed at Lambeth to deal with such cases."

These quotations from the licence officially issued by the Bishop of Long Island to the priest, Enrico Count di Campello, will sufficiently explain his present ecclesiastical *status*.

Thirdly, as to the work that he is doing. It has been confined this winter to Mission school work, to preaching and vesper services on Thursday and Sundays, at which a translation of the order for Evening Prayer of the Church of England has been used. He was unwilling to establish a proper cult — Eucharistic worship — without Episcopal authorisation. This work was done partly in the Ghetto, as a Mission to the Jews, and partly in some obscure rooms in the Via Farini, beyond S. Maria Maggiore. It has been purely evangelic work, everything in the nature of controversy being banished from it. It was hard drudgery among the lower classes of the people, with no encouragement almost save that of faith. What a contrast to the ecclesiastical life and work of St. Peter's, given up by the Count di Campello for truth's sake ! It was needful, however, and has been very useful as a spiritual discipline and a strengthening preparation for better things. It was carried on under the general direction of, and has been so far supported by, a self-constituted local committee, on which the Rev. C. R. Conybeare, the Rev. F. V. Thornton, and the Rev. J. Hill Tait represented actively the clergy of the Church of England.

It has now seemed time to take a step forward and place the Count di Campello in a position in which he can reach his fellow-citizens more widely, and those also of a better class. He has just taken a large and handsome hall in a central part of the city (No. 54, Via Nazionale). This will be fitted up as a provisional chapel, and divine worship be henceforth regularly celebrated therein. There are connected with it good rooms for school purposes. Two other priests— ex-monks—have been taken in as assistants to the Count di Campello in this part of the work—men who have for years endured much hardness for the truth's sake; men, too, who in character and instruction stand much above the average Roman priest.

About £600 sterling are needed to sustain this movement for the year. The committee has in hand means for less than two months. Heretofore the whole thing was so tentative, that I did not feel prepared to make any general appeal for help, and the expenses have been met by what the committee could give themselves or raise from their personal friends. But now the movement has been placed upon such solid foundations, and brought into such regular relations to the ecclesiastical authority, and promises to do such real service in this country, that I no longer hesitate to appeal to the Church Catholic for prompt and liberal support. Only those who have been much in Italy, and seen for themselves the distressing exile from Christianity to which the Papal Church relentlessly condemns everything which is most earnest and enlightened and patriotic in the manhood of this nation, can understand what a haven of rest a National Church, reformed and truly Catholic, will open to this sorely tempted people, and how many souls may be saved to Christ thereby.

From the Italian Government and people, if the movement takes hold, much can in time be expected, but not in its beginning. They who are strong, who are able, must first *lift*, at least, the burden of those who are weak—must help them to help themselves. For this year, at least, all support must be sought from outside. " Whoso hath this world's good, and seeth his brother have need, and shutteth up his compassion from him, how dwelleth the love of God in him ? "

R. J. NEVIN.

St. Paul's Church, Rome, May 24, 1883.

APPENDIX C.

Dr. Nevin's letter, which appeared in the *Guardian* on the second day of January, 1884, says :—

" Mgr. Savarese resigned his office as a Domestic Prelate of the Pope, professed his belief in the Nicene faith, renounced as not of the Catholic faith the corrupt additions made thereto by Popes Pius IV. and Pius IX., declared his belief in the Catholic character and authority of the Anglican Episcopate, and asked its guidance and protection against the uncatholic usurpations of the Bishop of Rome; but he did not leave the Catholic Church in Italy, nor did he join the American Church.

" He received at my hands the Holy Eucharist, partly in witness of his belief in the Catholicity of our communion, and partly because the present Bishop of Rome has forbidden his priests to give the sacrament to those who will not defile the faith once given to the saints with his unholy additions.

" His application for Episcopal guidance was made to the Archbishop of Canterbury as head of the Commission appointed by the Lambeth Conference in 1878 to deal with such cases. His Grace, for reasons of convenience, has referred it to the Bishop in charge of the American chapels on the continent of Europe, in like manner as the application of the Count di Campello was referred to the same Bishop by Archbishop Tait. Thus Mgr. Savarese will work for the restoration of the primitive faith and Catholic order in the Church of Italy, under due Episcopal guidance and protection.

" His act in renouncing the Papal obedience, taken after long and painful consideration, without bitterness or personal disappointment, must carry with it great weight, for he is a man in the fullest vigour of his powers, and one of the very foremost canonists and theologians in the Roman Curia.

" The considerations which seem to have been chief in leading him to the decisive step that he has taken were, firstly, the great spiritual destitution of the Italian people under the false shepherding of the Papacy, and the woeful loss of souls resulting therefrom ; and, secondly, the insurmountable obstacle opposed by the Papacy to the reunion of Christendom ; and this last fact led him, in a closer study of history, to recognise in the Papacy the great author of schism in the Church from the beginning.

" R. J. NEVIN."

APPENDIX D.

From the GUARDIAN *of October* 22, 1884.

CATHOLIC REFORM IN ITALY.

SIR,—May I be allowed to answer through your columns many questioners in regard to the present position of the Catholic reform work in Italy under the direction of Monsignore Savarese and the Count di Campello?

1.—I find on my return to Rome that the chapel started by them in the Via Genoa has distinctly gained ground forward during the summer. The congregation has increased in numbers and in regularity of attendance; the entire absence of foreigners from Rome during the summer has relieved the priests in charge from a somewhat distracting force in the services, and enabled them to develop more efficiently the natural Italian elements. They tell me that they have now more than a dozen children in preparation for confirmation, and that they are most anxious for the help and encouragement of an immediate Episcopal visitation.

2.—The formal excommunication launched by the Pope on the 29th September against all the members of this congregation has given them a great lift, and they may indeed sing with David, "Though they curse, yet bless Thou." It has not frightened away a single member of their usual congregation; but it has drawn to their services many new hearers. It has made their hopes and efforts known to thousands all over Italy, who otherwise might never have heard of them, and it has generally awakened a kindly disposition towards them. Many letters have come in from priests all over Italy, who, even if they are not so situated as to be able to cast in their lot at once with this open movement for reform, yet hearing these things, wish to say that they thank God and take courage.

The press all over Italy has been led to take notice of the stand now making for Catholic reform, and an opening has thus come for a statement of its true principles and aims to be brought before the Italian people, in the way of an apology, in answer to the Cardinal-Vicar's lengthy and somewhat confused arraignment. And this can be done with the more effect, since his Eminence, in the heat of his anger, not only indulged in an amount of vituperation little becoming in the representative of the professed representative of Christ, but also made some statements in regard to the teachings and worship of these Italian Catholics which, in point of fact, are simply not true. This will become apparent at once, on the publication at the end of this week of their *Liturgia*—a translation into Italian of the Latin Missal, with only so much of revision as was necessary to bring it into agreement with Catholic teaching and practice which has been in use in their services since Monsignore Savarese took charge of this Mission. The Cardinal-Vicar, having been somewhat premature in the fulmination just launched, will have to forge a separate bolt for this service-book.

In the providence of God a great opportunity has thus been given, through the violence of their enemies, to those who are working for reform in Italy. I pray that they may have grace given them to use it wisely, and that their brethren in England and America, who hold dear the faith once delivered to the saints, and the one Holy Catholic and Apostolic Church, will come to their help willingly in providing the material means necessary to carry on efficiently their work.

R. J. NEVIN.

St. Paul's Church, Rome, October 15, 1884.

APPENDIX E.

From the GUARDIAN *of Nov.* 19, 1884.

THE LITURGIES OF THE ITALIAN CATHOLIC CHURCH.

SIR—In answer to requests for further information in regard to the *Liturgia* of the Italian Catholic Church, may I be allowed to say that it is a translation into Italian of the Roman Missal, with barely so much revision as was necessary to restore its earlier Catholic features—*i.e.*, the Holy Communion is given in both kinds, the few passages which teach the invocation and intercession of saints have been thoroughly eliminated and the words "*mysterium fidei*," intruded into our Lord's institution for the consecration of the cup, have been removed? Besides the feasts retained in the Church of England, there are special offices for those of St. Joseph, St. Ambrose, the Conception, and the passing away of the Blessed Virgin, and for the feast of the patron saint of the particular church. The table of Scripture Lessons of the Church of England for Matins and Vespers is printed with the Missal.

The Cardinal-Vicar, in making up his case of heresy against this Italian Catholic movement, had not seen their Office. He got hold of an Italian translation of the English Evensong, provisionally used in their worship, of M. Hyacinthe Loyson's service-book, which had never been used, and of a collection of Italian psalms and hymns issued by the Wesleyan Mission, I believe, and which was used in *their choir,* as they could find no other hymns set to music, but was *not in the hands of the congregation.* From this the Cardinal selected two hymns which *had never been sung in their church ;* from the English Office he picked out the form of absolution ; and on these grounds, together with certain portions of M. Loyson's book, he made out his case of *heresy.* Now, the only one of his charges which by any possibility can be held as true against the Italian Catholic Church is its use of the form of absolution which is used every morning and evening in the Church of England : this, and the fact that they " *hold the schismatic Orientals and the Anglicans to belong to the true Church."* What is one to think of a Pope who solemnly condemns everlastingly a great number of human souls—for his curse rests upon every person that enters their chapel—upon every one who assists them in every way, upon every one who prints a notice of their services, or reports their sermons or lectures—and formally makes up his judgment with such criminal inexactness?

The answer to the Cardinal-Vicar's excommunication just issued and signed " for the Italian Catholic Church " by Mgr. Savarese, the Count di Campello, and two other priests is a truly remarkable paper. Without a single angry or disrespectful word, it meets the accusation of schism with the answer that the Pope is not the Holy Catholic Church, that its government was given to the universal Episcopate, in which all Bishops, according to St. Cyprian and St Jerome, were equal, and that in the present lapse of the Italian Bishops, they have their sufficient mission to preach the Gospel as Christ gave it, and administer the sacraments as He commanded from that part of the Episcopate which had stood fast in the faith and discipline of the Catholic Church. Against the charge of heresy is given the answer that they hold the faith of the undivided Church, the "*quod semper*," &c., of St. Vincent, a master not yet condemned by the *Curia Romana*, that the Vatican additions are not to be found in the Gospels, which contain all that is necessary to salvation, and that the Pope, as the author of unwarranted additions to the faith, has exposed himself to the condemnation of the Councils of Ephesus and Chalcedon. Standing as to the faith with the primitive Church they can smile at the nightmare of heresy, and remaining united to antiquity they cannot be divided from the Catholic Church. Every paper that I have seen has spoken favourably of this "Apology," both as to its spirit and the reasonableness of its argument.

R. J. NEVIN.

St. Paul's Church, Rome, October 25, 1884.

APPENDIX F.

Dr. Nevin's reply to GUARDIAN *attack, not printed by that paper.*

SIR,—I was very sorry indeed to see in the *Guardian* of Oct. 29 that your esteemed Paris correspondent should have gone far out of his way to lend himself to an anonymous, and as you assure your readers a libellous attack upon the Italian Catholic Reform movement in Rome. I have been asked by a well-known English clergyman to notice his remarks, inasmuch as he had spread abroad the accusation of "serious charges" against the "origin and character" of this movement, even though the anonymous statement of which he did not think it unbecoming his responsible position, as your leading foreign correspondent, to make himself the vehicle, was not published on account of its libellous character. I have, therefore, first of all, to ask him to send me a copy of the statement referred to in his remarks. If any charges are seriously made against this movement, I certainly desire most earnestly to be informed of them, and I will do my best to investigate them fully and fairly, both in my own defence and in justice to those who may have been led by my representations to assist it. I venture to think that your Paris correspondent owes it to his reputation for fairness and good faith to communicate to me this statement without hesitation, the more so as I will promise, under these circumstances, not to prosecute his papal friend for libel.

I know, of course, that very serious charges were made three years ago against the Count di Campello, one of the leading spirits in the Italian Catholic Movement. I went to great pains at that time, with the assistance of several English clergymen then in Rome, to examine into the truth of these charges. I questioned in the matter a number of Roman prelates, who were in a position to know intimately the past life of Campello, the heads of the Roman police, and the most important among the foreign correspondents who had carelessly allowed themselves to spread abroad these charges in their letters. I found that no proof was produced in support of any really serious charge that would have been admitted for a moment in any civilised court of justice. The charges themselves were based upon generally vague, and always anonymous accusations, and the most serious of them referred to events that had happened a good many years ago, previous to very high promotion given by Pope Pius IX himself to the Count di Campello. All this was reported by me at length in an article, entitled "A Notable Secession from the Vatican," published in the *Nineteenth Century*, April, 1882.

But I have yet to hear that any charge, affecting his honour or personal character, has been made against Monsignore Savarese. Certainly nothing of the kind has appeared openly here in Rome, and I, therefore, naturally mistrust somewhat this anonymous "statement" which its author wanted to smuggle into the columns of the *Guardian*, but has been afraid to put forth in Rome. It is certain that their enemies bear a most "tyrannous hate" against these two men, in proportion to the courage and constancy that they have shown in withstanding, as long as they have, the threats and blandishments of the Roman Curia. Blandishments certainly as well as threats, because even since the greater excommunication launched against them, great efforts have been made to woo them back to outward submission to the Papacy, even an Archbishop stooping to act as the direct agent of the Vatican's flatteries and promises. There can be no question at all, that, notwithstanding all the mud flung at them, they would to-day be received back with rewards far more substantial than those which, chiefly in the hope of influencing them, have been given to Padre Curci since his technical submission. And, on the other hand, they have lately been given clearly to understand that if they persist longer in their protest for the Catholic traditions of the Church, every possible force will be put forth to crush them, and no mercy will be shown. For the Vatican is now thoroughly roused and alarmed by the little cloud that has begun to gather on the horizon of this spiritually famished land, and sees in it a danger, which the Pope is said

D

to have characterized as greater than any that Protestantism has threatened in Italy.

Further, as your Paris correspondent, although admitting that he has no information in the case, has seen fit to judge my letter in your correspondence of October 22nd, to be an *ex-parte* statement, I feel it necessary to add that I have all along declined to assume any official relation to this movement, and that I have no possible personal interest to serve in defending its leaders. It calls for no little personal sacrifice indeed to stand for them here in Rome. The little that I have been able to do to help them has made me not a few enemies, and cost me both money and time that I could ill afford in the already excessively heavy demands made upon me by my duties as Chaplain, but I cannot, as I love the Lord Jesus Christ, stand by and see fall to the ground for want of a little timely sympathy and help, the only movement that has arisen in these days in Italy, which seems to me to carry with it any reasonable hope of reclaiming this people to His religion. I say reclaim, advisedly, without any intention of disrespect to those many Roman Catholics who devoutly cling to the Chistian faith within the Papal obedience, because it is an undoubted fact that, quite apart from the widespread infidelity that has eaten deep into the vitals of the Roman Church, the larger part of the Italian people have strayed away, not only from that Church, but from the Christian faith itself as acknowledged in any dogmatic form. No faithful Roman Catholic will question this fact, I presume, as it has formed the burden of frequent Papal denunciations since the year 1870. Now though the cry of these spiritual estrays may not yet be very bitter—for poor souls, they do not yet realize their own great want and danger—yet the sight of them, wandering off farther and farther into

the thorny tangle of rationalism, or the foodless
deserts of materialism, is very piteous to those of us
who being on the ground must see it. There is no
power in the Roman Church to call them back. The
make-shift folds to which they are diligently called by
the many Protestant missions recently started in Italy
seem to them unattractive and cold and foodless;
moreover, built as they largely are on plans of man's
devising, it may be at least questioned whether they
offer a shelter that is wholly safe, and that will be
permanent. These lost sheep this Italian Catholic movement, as already declared from the beginning, is seeking,
and I see no hope of saving for them in any other quarter.

There is another fact in regard to these Italian
Catholics which, though it has not the compelling
power of conscience to move to interest in their behalf,
is yet one which will strike a chord of sympathy in
every Englishman among your readers who has not
been denationalized by long exposure to Latin associa-
tions, and that is that they are fighting a singularly
brave fight for what they believe to be truth, at fearful
odds, against enemies who do not know what it is to
fight fair, and who have not one spark of generosity in
them. These men are few in numbers, undisciplined,
untrained, poor, and absolutely without political or
social influence. The Papacy cannot, it is true, since
1870, fight its spiritual battles with the brute force of
the temporal power, informing conscience by the
dungeons and faggots of the Inquisition, but its power
in this country in material things is still incredibly
great. It has, practically, unlimited supplies of money
and well-trained men. It has enormous social influence.
It has powerful political influence in high quarters. It
has the press, both native and foreign, very largely at its
disposal. It has in Rome to-day, as over against these
men, pretty much everything on its side except truth.

And it uses its resources unscrupulously. To all this must be added the fact that the Infidelity of Italy hates and fears, even more than it does Romanism, any reform that stands firm upon the foundations of primitive Christianity, and is always ready to lend a helping hand to the superstition of Italy, in strangling any truly Catholic movement. For these reasons these men have not really been able to get a hearing in Italy until now, when their opportunity has come through the unprovoked attack made upon them by the Pope, in his recent savage and most unchristian excommunication.

R. J. NEVIN.

St. Paul's Church, Rome, Nov. 5, 1884.